PERTH UNION LIBRARY

D1542749

FOR THE CHILDREN OF SAWREY
FROM
OLD MR. BUNNY

FREDERICK WARNE

Published by the Penguin Group
Registered office: 80 Strand, London, WC2R ORL
Penguin Young Readers Group, 345 Hudson Street, New York, N.Y. 10014, USA

First published 1904 by Frederick Warne
This edition with new reproductions of Beatrix Potter's book illustrations first published 2006
This edition copyright © Frederick Warne & Co. 2006
New reproductions of Beatrix Potter's book illustrations copyright © Frederick Warne & Co. 2002
Original copyright in text and illustrations © Frederick Warne & Co., 1904

Manufactured in China

THE TALE OF
BENJAMIN BUNNY

BY BEATRIX POTTER

FREDERICK WARNE

ONE morning a little rabbit sat on a bank.
He pricked his ears and listened to the
trit-trot, trit-trot of a pony.

A gig was coming along the road; it was
driven by Mr. McGregor, and beside him
sat Mrs. McGregor in her best bonnet.

AS soon as they had passed, little Benjamin
Bunny slid down into the road, and set off—
with a hop, skip and a jump—to call upon his
relations, who lived in the wood at the back
of Mr. McGregor's garden.

THAT wood was full of rabbit-holes; and in the neatest sandiest hole of all, lived Benjamin's aunt and his cousins—Flopsy, Mopsy, Cotton-tail and Peter.

Old Mrs. Rabbit was a widow; she earned her living by knitting rabbit-wool mittens and muffetees (I once bought a pair at a bazaar). She also sold herbs, and rosemary tea, and rabbit-tobacco (which is what *we* call lavender).

LITTLE Benjamin did not very much want
to see his Aunt.

He came round the back of the fir-tree, and
nearly tumbled upon the top of his Cousin
Peter.

PETER was sitting by himself. He looked poorly, and was dressed in a red cotton pocket-handkerchief.

"Peter,"—said little Benjamin, in a whisper— "who has got your clothes?"

PETER replied—"The scarecrow in Mr. McGregor's garden," and described how he had been chased about the garden, and had dropped his shoes and coat.

Little Benjamin sat down beside his cousin, and assured him that Mr. McGregor had gone out in a gig, and Mrs. McGregor also; and certainly for the day, because she was wearing her best bonnet.

PETER said he hoped that it would rain.

At this point, old Mrs. Rabbit's voice was heard inside the rabbit hole, calling—"Cotton-tail! Cotton-tail! Fetch some more camomile!"

Peter said he thought he might feel better if he went for a walk.

THEY went away hand in hand, and got upon the flat top of the wall at the bottom of the wood. From here they looked down into Mr. McGregor's garden. Peter's coat and shoes were plainly to be seen upon the scarecrow, topped with an old tam-o-shanter of Mr. McGregor's.

LITTLE Benjamin said, "It spoils people's clothes to squeeze under a gate; the proper way to get in, is to climb down a pear tree."

Peter fell down head first; but it was of no consequence, as the bed below was newly raked and quite soft.

IT had been sown with lettuces.
  They left a great many odd little foot-marks
all over the bed, especially little Benjamin, who
was wearing clogs.

LITTLE Benjamin said that the first thing
to be done was to get back Peter's clothes, in
order that they might be able to use the pocket-
handkerchief.

They took them off the scarecrow. There had
been rain during the night; there was water in
the shoes, and the coat was somewhat shrunk.

Benjamin tried on the tam-o-shanter, but it
was too big for him.

THEN he suggested that they should fill the pocket handkerchief with onions, as a little present for his Aunt.

Peter did not seem to be enjoying himself; he kept hearing noises.

BENJAMIN, on the contrary, was perfectly at home, and ate a lettuce leaf. He said that he was in the habit of coming to the garden with his father to get lettuces for their Sunday dinner.

(The name of little Benjamin's papa was old Mr. Benjamin Bunny.)

The lettuces certainly were very fine.

PETER did not eat anything; he said he should like to go home. Presently he dropped half the onions.

LITTLE Benjamin said that it was not possible to get back up the peartree, with a load of vegetables. He led the way boldly towards the other end of the garden. They went along a little walk on planks, under a sunny red-brick wall.

The mice sat on their door-steps cracking cherry-stones, they winked at Peter Rabbit and little Benjamin Bunny.

Presently Peter let the pocket-handkerchief go again.

THEY got amongst flower-pots, and frames and tubs; Peter heard noises worse than ever, his eyes were as big as lolly-pops!

He was a step or two in front of his cousin, when he suddenly stopped.

THIS is what those little rabbits saw round that corner!

Little Benjamin took one look, and then, in half a minute less than no time, he hid himself and Peter and the onions underneath a large basket. . . .

THE cat got up and stretched herself, and came and sniffed at the basket.

Perhaps she liked the smell of onions!

Anyway, she sat down upon the top of the basket.

She sat there for *five hours*.

*   *   *   *   *

I cannot draw you a picture of Peter and Benjamin underneath the basket, because it was quite dark, and because the smell of onions was fearful; it made Peter Rabbit and little Benjamin cry.

The sun got round behind the wood, and it was quite late in the afternoon; but still the cat sat upon the basket.

AT length
there was a
pitter-patter,
pitter-patter,
and some bits
of mortar fell
from the wall
above.
The cat
looked up and
saw old Mr.
Benjamin Bunny
prancing along the
top of the wall of the
upper terrace.

He was smoking a pipe of rabbit-tobacco,
and had a little switch in his hand.

He was looking for his son.

OLD Mr. Bunny had no opinion whatever of cats.

He took a tremendous jump off the top of the wall on to the top of the cat, and cuffed it off the basket, and kicked it into the green-house, scratching off a handful of fur.

The cat was too much surprised to scratch back.

WHEN old Mr. Bunny had driven the cat
into the green-house, he locked the door.
Then he came back to the basket and took
out his son Benjamin by the ears, and whipped
him with the little switch.

Then he took out his
nephew Peter.

Then he took
out the
handkerchief
of onions,
and marched
out of the
garden.

WHEN Mr. McGregor returned about half an hour later, he observed several things which perplexed him.

It looked as though some person had been walking all over the garden in a pair of clogs — only the foot-marks were too ridiculously little!

Also he could not understand how the cat could have managed to shut herself up *inside* the green-house, locking the door upon the *outside*.

WHEN Peter got home, his mother forgave him, because she was so glad to see that he had found his shoes and coat. Cotton-tail and Peter folded up the pocket-handkerchief, and old Mrs. Rabbit strung up the onions and hung them from the kitchen ceiling, with the bunches of herbs and the rabbit-tobacco.